My Grandpa's
BATTLESHIP MISSOURI TOUR

My Grandpa's

BATTLESHIP
MISSOURI
TOUR

written & illustrated by Jeff Langcaon

MUTUAL PUBLISHING

This book is dedicated to all those who proudly
served aboard the USS *Missouri*, and especially to
Grandpa Toby, who first signed aboard her crew
more than fifty years ago, and who still proudly
leads tours across her decks today.

Library of Congress Cataloging-in-Publication Data

Langcaon, Jeff.
    My grandpa's Battleship Missouri tour / written & illustrated by Jeff Langcaon.
        p. cm.
    Summary: During career month at school, a young boy's grandfather volunteers to show the class
around the USS Missouri and explain how he was stationed on the ship that played a big part in history.
    ISBN-13: 978-1-56647-831-1 (hardcover : alk. paper)
    ISBN-10: 1-56647-831-6 (hardcover : alk. paper)
    [1. Schools--Fiction. 2. Grandfathers--Fiction. 3. Missouri (Battleship : BB 63)--Fiction. 4. Stories in rhyme.]
I. Title.
PZ8.3.L27673My 2007
[E]--dc22
                                          2007013039

ISBN-10: 1-56647-831-6
ISBN-13: 978-1-56647-831-1

First Printing, October 2007

Mutual Publishing, LLC
1215 Center Street, Suite 210
Honolulu, Hawai'i 96816
Ph: 808-732-1709 / Fax: 808-734-4094
email: info@mutualpublishing.com
www.mutualpublishing.com

Printed in China

"Attention class, please,"
We heard Miss Lovett say
As we sat at our desks
At the start of the day.

"This month," said our teacher,
"You will learn something new.
We'll find out all about
Different jobs people do."

"So I'd like to invite
Moms and dads to come share
About places they work
And the things they do there."

"I will give you a note
For your parents to see.
Have them fill it all out
Then return it to me."

I put that note safely
in my bag out of sight,
And forgot all about it
Till Mom found it that night.

It's

CAREER MONTH!

Hey Moms and Dads!

Moms and Dads, please help us learn all about the many different and interesting jobs that people do, and what happens there! types of places that people work, and what happens there! You can sign up to come speak to our class about your career, or you can invite another family member to share their experience with us!

If you would like to help our class learn about careers, please fill out the bottom portion of this form, and return it to me.

THANK YOU!

HOMEROOM _____

STUDENT NAME _____

☐ Yes! I would like to come and speak about a career!

☐ No, I won't be able to make it.

NAME _____

When my mom read the note,
She made a small frown.
"I'm so busy this month,
And your dad's out-of-town."

Then she nodded her head
And said, "Why, I know!
I can call and we'll ask
Your grandfather to go."

Now, my grandpa is cool.
We have fun when we play.
But I didn't think
He'd have too much to say.

After all, he's retired,
And I never asked
About jobs Grandpa had
Way, way back in the past.

But before I could speak,
Mom had made a phone call.
Then she said, "It's all set!
Don't you worry at all."

"Grandpa's happy to go.
He'll be glad to go speak."
So, I had no worries
Till the following week.

That Monday, Kay's mom
Was the first to appear.
She talked of her job as
A software engineer.

Pono's dad came on Tuesday
And he told us about
His job as a fireman
Putting big fires out.

When Wednesday came around,
That was my Grandpa's day.
But I had no idea
What he was going to say.

The morning bell rang.
Grandpa wasn't there yet.
I thought, "Oh, no! I hope
Grandpa didn't forget."

Then Miss Lovett said, "Class,
There's a real treat for us.
It's a field trip today,
So let's go board our bus."

While we rode on that bus
Everyone laughed and joked
With no clue where we were,
Until our teacher spoke:

"Settle down children—our
Destination is near.
I can see the big ships
In Pearl Harbor from here."

"When we get there, we'll take
Quite a special trip.
We'll be getting a tour
Of a great battleship."

"USS *Missouri*
Is this famous ship's name.
We will learn of its past
And hear tales of its fame."

We rode to Ford Island.
My class gathered dockside,
Standing in a big group
Waiting for our tour guide.

There were colorful state flags
That we walked between,
Leading up to the biggest
Ship I'd ever seen.

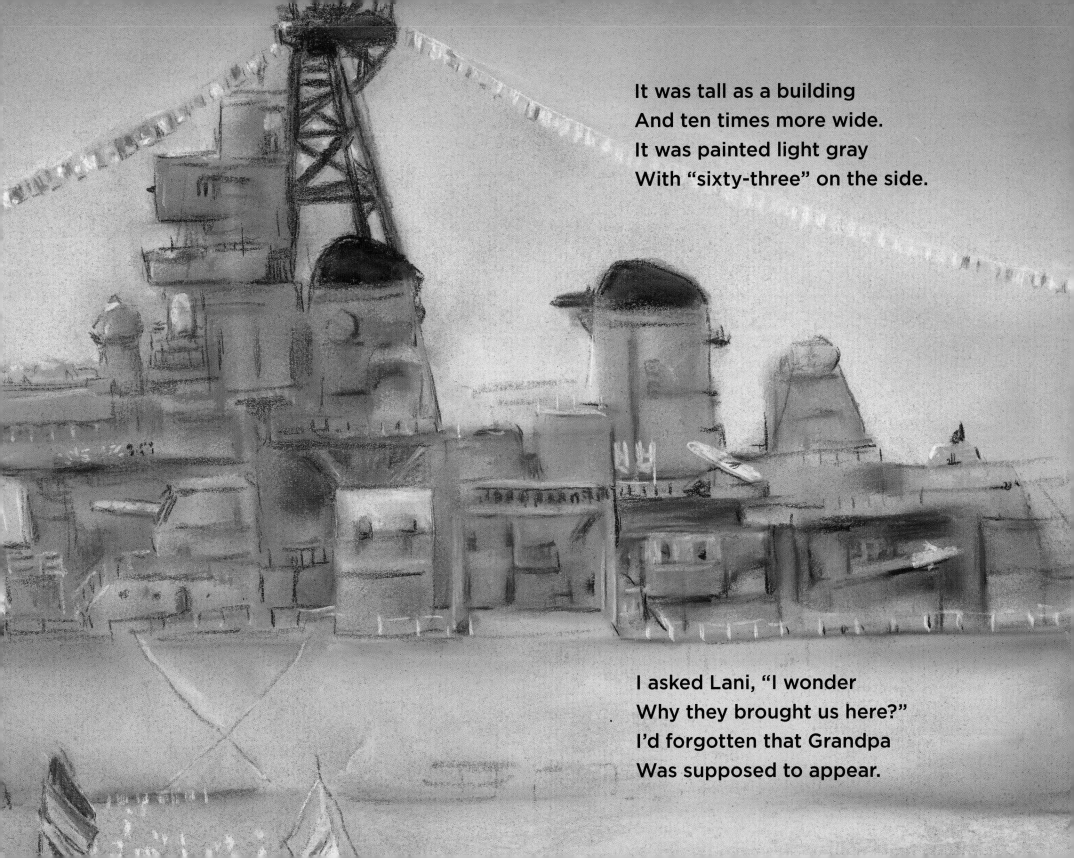

It was tall as a building
And ten times more wide.
It was painted light gray
With "sixty-three" on the side.

I asked Lani, "I wonder
Why they brought us here?"
I'd forgotten that Grandpa
Was supposed to appear.

Then our tour guide arrived.
I felt my face turn red
When I recognized him.
"That's my grandpa!" I said.

"Grandpa, I never knew
You were a sailor before."
He nodded and laughed.
"I was that and much more."

Then he turned to the class
And said, "I'm glad to see
You could all come to tour
My old workplace with me."

"I know you'll have fun
And learn lots on our trip.
USS *Missouri*
Is an amazing ship."

"She's special for quite a
Few reasons, it's true.
Come this way and I'll share
Something real cool with you."

"On this board are old pictures
Of some of her crew."
He pointed to one boy,
Smiled, and asked us, "Guess who?"

"Is that YOU?" Lani asked.
"Well, it was way back when
I was younger," said Grandpa,
"And had more hair back then."

"But enough about me.
You're all ready, I'm sure.
Let's board the Missouri
For the start of your tour."

Grandpa led us on deck.
We posed under the guns.
"Each outweighs the Space Shuttle—
Over one hundred tons."

"These big guns are so large
That I've heard sailors say
They could shoot at a target
Twenty-three miles away!"

"This ship's built with thick steel;
Its design is unique.
Why, this deck underfoot
Is wood boards made of teak."

Then we went below deck.
"Watch your step and your head.
You don't want to bump into
These doors," Grandpa said.

He showed us the small bunks
Where the sailors would sleep,
All stacked top to bottom,
Four and five sailors deep.

"Now this ship is empty,
But was full, way back when.
In 'forty-five she held
Twenty-seven hundred men."

"They all lived onboard ship
Perhaps six months or more.
So right here is a laundry,
And the ship's general store."

"There was a barber down here
Who would cut the men's hair,
A bakery, and mess hall,
To feed them all there."

Next we toured the control room.
The class squeezed in to fit.
We took turns in the chair
Where the captain would sit.

Grandpa said, "Let's go out,
For before you all go,
There's an important part
Of our ship still to show."

"The Missouri is not just
A battleship, you see;
She played a large role
In U.S. history."

"In nineteen forty-five
On a September day,
She sailed with our allies
Into Tokyo Bay."

"On this very deck
It was this spot they chose
As the place they would bring
World War Two to a close."

"All the countries that fought
In the war came to meet,
And the Japanese forces
Acknowledged defeat."

"A peace treaty was signed.
The war came to an end,
And the wounds from that conflict
Could soon start to mend."

"So she's here to remind us:
We would truly regret
If the lessons of history
We should ever forget."

"Now we've come to the end.
I've had fun, to be sure.
Now it's time for goodbye,
Hope you enjoyed our tour."

My class all applauded.
Pono asked Grandpa, "When
Can we all come back and
Tour Missouri again?"

Grandpa smiled. "Come back soon!
There's still much more to tell.
Why, next time you should bring
Your whole family as well."

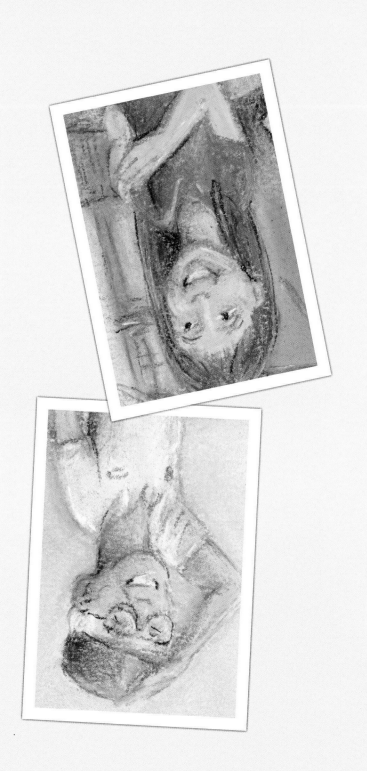

Kay said, "I wish MY grandpa
Did stuff like this too."
"Bet he does," Grandpa said,
"But, it's all up to you."

"You should ask your grandparents
Of things that they've done.
You might learn stuff from them
That's exciting and fun."

Then we hugged, and he said
"Glad you had fun today."
The class waved and yelled "Bye!"
As our bus drove away.

He had showed us his ship,
Told us what she could do.
He was proud of that ship.
I was proud of him too.

It was cool to find out
What MY grandpa could do.
When you get the chance,
Ask YOUR grandparents too!